Terrific
Toddlers

Potty!

by Carol Zeavin, MSEd, MEd
and Rhona Silverbush, JD

illustrated by Jon Davis

Magination Press • Washington, DC • American Psychological Association

Magination Press

Books for Kids From the
American Psychological Association

Text copyright © 2020 by Carol Zeavin and Rhona Silverbush.
Illustrations copyright © 2020 by Jon Davis. Published in 2020
by Magination Press, an imprint of the American Psychological
Association. All rights reserved. Except as permitted under the
United States Copyright Act of 1976, no part of this publication
may be reproduced or distributed in any form or by any means, or
stored in a database or retrieval system, without the prior written
permission of the publisher.

Magination Press is a registered trademark of the American Psychological Association. Order books at maginationpress.org,
or call 1-800-374-2721.

Book design by Gwen Grafft
Printed by Worzalla, Stevens Point, WI

Library of Congress Cataloging-in-Publication Data
Names: Zeavin, Carol, author. | Silverbush, Rhona, 1967- author. |
    Davis, Jon, 1969- illustrator.
Title: Potty! / by Carol Zeavin, MSEd, MEd and Rhona Silverbush,
    JD ; illustrated by Jon Davis.
Description: Washington, DC : Magination Press, 2020. | Series:
    Terrific toddlers | "American Psychological Association." |
    Audience: Ages 2-3. | Audience: Grades K-1. | Summary:
    "Sometimes we make pee-pee, sometimes we make poopy. When
    we are ready, we all use the potty"— Provided by publisher.
Identifiers: LCCN 2019043245 | ISBN 9781433832512 (hardcover)
Subjects: LCSH: Toilet training—Juvenile literature.
Classification: LCC HQ770.5 .Z43 2020 | DDC 649/.62—dc23
LC record available at https://lccn.loc.gov/2019043245

Manufactured in the United States of America
10 9 8 7 6 5 4 3 2 1

With gratitude to my inspiring teachers and mentors
at Bank Street, Rockefeller, and Barnard—*CZ*

Dedicated to the inspiration for this series
(you know who you are!), with infinite love—*RS*

For Laura and Greta—*JD*

More Terrific Toddlers

Sometimes we make pee-pee, sometimes we make poopy.
Are we ready to use the potty?

JoJo does NOT want to use the potty—
but she does not like her diaper wet!
Today, she is squishing some play dough.

Suddenly, she stops.
"Mommy, Mommy!" she says. "I do pee-pee!"

Mommy says, "OK, let's go change your wet diaper."

JoJo yells, "Take it off! Take it off!"
She starts to pull her diaper down...

Mommy says, "We take off diapers
in the bathroom, please!
I'll help you...."

Kai has fun sitting on his potty—with all of his clothes on!
Today, he makes a poopy in his diaper while he sits.

When Kai's done and wiped,
Daddy puts the poopy in the toilet.
Kai says, "I flush it."
He pushes the handle...

Whoosh! goes the water. "AAAH!" Kai yells.
"I know," Daddy says.
"The water takes away your poopy—but not you!"

Kai waves. "Bye-bye, poopy!"

Jack likes to make pee-pee and poopy in the potty.
Today, he is reading a book while he sits.

Mommy peeks in.
"Did something come out?"

Jack stands up and looks.
"Pee-pee!" he says. "No poopy."

He sits down again. He reads some more.

He stands up and looks.
"No poopy, Mommy."

"That's OK," Mommy says. "You tried."
Jack nods. "Yup!"

Ava doesn't wear a diaper anymore—
and she loves her flowered underwear!

Today, she's helping Daddy water the plants.
All of a sudden, she feels pee-pee coming.
"Uh-oh!" she says, "Pee-pee!"

"That's OK," Daddy says.
"You're learning to use the potty."
Ava says, "I do potty!!"

We all make pee-pee and poopy.
And when we're ready, we use the potty!

Note to Parents and Caregivers

Your child is ready to potty train! Or so you wish.

While the transition from diapers to independence can be very exciting for everyone involved, it can also be truly fraught for parents. We get it. Diapers are expensive, grandparents are nagging, friends' children are sporting superhero underwear. You'd love to get to the other side—that side where your child uses the toilet independently. But the bridge from here to there seems long and rickety...

This process will be easier if you understand that your child is the one to build the bridge! It will also be easier if you understand that your child needs two things to be in place:

Physical readiness: Children need to be able to feel the sensations of needing to pee and poop, understand what the sensations mean, and control the muscles that hold in and let go. This takes neurological development that happens at different rates for different children (you can assure Grandma that it has absolutely nothing to do with intelligence!).

Emotional readiness: At the same time, children need to be able to understand what's expected of them, and to follow step-by-step instructions. Sometimes, they must also overcome fears—of the elimination process itself (what other parts of me will fall out?!), or of the toilet and its loud flush, the gush of water that could suck them down along with their poop.

Some ways you will know their bridge-building has begun:

- They seek out squishy substances like play dough and mud;
- They find a way to tell you they are noticing full or wet diapers;
- They become obsessively curious about others' toileting habits;
- They stay dry longer;
- They start refusing diapers.

To help them build their bridge...

...it's best not to:

- Compare your child with others;
- Equate potty training with maturity;
- Punish accidents—your child really can't help it;
- Overdo prizes—their own accomplishment is their biggest reward.

...and it's best to:

- Stay calm and matter-of-fact;
- Be prepared for accidents;
- Expect variation—sometimes something will come out, sometimes it won't... two steps forward, one step back...

They may shout "No!" a lot, but your children do actually want your approval, and they know you want them to use the potty. Eventually they will gain mastery over their bodily functions, and they will be as pleased and proud as you are. Remember—barring a disability that prevents it, every person becomes potty-trained. Your child will, too!

We love toddler pronunciation! And we know toddlers are not yet able to pronounce the complicated consonants in "flush." We just didn't want to annoy you with an approximated spelling of most toddlers' best efforts ("I f'uth it," "I fwuss it"). So, don't worry if your toddler can't pronounce "flush" the way Kai does—Kai can't, either!

A note about the terms "pee-pee" and "poopy": We've chosen these terms, because that's what we've used with the toddlers in our own lives, but please feel free to substitute whichever terms your toddler is familiar with while enjoying the book together.

Carol Zeavin holds master's degrees in education and special education from Bank Street College, and worked for eighteen years in homes and classrooms with toddlers. She was Head Teacher at both Rockefeller University's Child and Family Center and at the Barnard Toddler Development Center, and worked for Y.A.I. and Theracare. She is a professional violinist living in New York, NY.

Rhona Silverbush studied psychology and theater at Brandeis University and law at Boston College Law School. She represented refugees and has written and co-written several books, including a guide to acting Shakespeare. She currently coaches actors, writes, tutors, and consults for families of children and teens with learning differences and special needs. She lives in New York, NY.

Visit terrifictoddlersbookseries.com

🐦 @CarolRhona

📷 @TerrificToddlersBooks

Jon Davis is an award-winning illustrator of more than 80 books. He lives in England.

Visit jonsmind.com

🐦 @JonDavisIllust

📷 @JonDavisIllustration

Magination Press is the children's book imprint of the American Psychological Association. Through APA's publications, the association shares with the world mental health expertise and psychological knowledge. Magination Press books reach young readers and their parents and caregivers to make navigating life's challenges a little easier. It's the combined power of psychology and literature that makes a Magination Press book special.

Visit www.maginationpress.org

ⓕ 🐦 📷 ⓟ @MaginationPress